AF207331

Emily's Tiger

by Penny Pollock

Illustrated by Judy Morgan

paulist press
new york/mahwah

For Alyce Pollock
who lives a life of faith.

Emily's Tiger had the lumps. He'd
been in a terrible quarrel with the
bulldog from across the street. The
dog shook Tiger till his stuffing
shifted. That's how Tiger got the
lumps. In that same quarrel, Tiger
lost his right arm, and the second of
his green glass eyes, and his stomach
was ripped till his insides showed. But
his lumps were the worst injury
because they made his stripes crooked.

Emily found him, and his right arm,
under the front porch. She wrapped
him in her favorite blanket and said,
"I told you it was dangerous to camp
out alone all night under the lilac
bush."

Tiger never said a thing, but he
looked sad enough for a thousand
words and Emily wished she hadn't
scolded.
"Don't worry, you'll be fixed," she
said, and set off to find help.

Her mother was cutting the grass. The
mower made so much noise that
Emily had to yell to be heard. "Look
what's happened to Tiger!"
Her mother stopped long enough to
say, "I guess that's the end of good
old Tiger," and went right on cutting
the grass.

Emily's father was shining his
policeman's shoes in the kitchen. She
held up Tiger's body and his arm, but
all her father said was, "So that
finishes tired old Tiger."

Emily's brother was washing their
dog, Roscoe, in the bathtub. "Can you
help fix Tiger?" Emily asked.
"No," he said. "Tiger's nothing but a
yellowed mothy rag. Besides, I have
to wash Roscoe. Do you want to
help?"
"No," said Emily. "I have to take
care of Tiger."
"If you help with Roscoe, I'll let you
help me take him to the Blessing of
the Animals in church tomorrow,"
her brother said.
"I don't have time," Emily answered
and rocked Tiger from side to side.
"Then you can't come with me to the
Blessing," her brother said and stuck
out his tongue.

But Emily did go to the Blessing. Her whole family went. Roscoe looked prancy with a new red ribbon on his tail.

Emily wore red, too, She wore her red raincoat with the big pockets.
"It's not raining," her brother said.
"It might," said Emily and walked backwards all the way to church just to prove she could.

When the service started, her brother
asked, "Aren't you going to take your
coat off?"
"No," Emily replied and studied the
flowery stars on the ceiling.

Her brother led Roscoe to the altar.
Roscoe behaved well for a dog.
BUT . . . . .

Two cats hissed. One pig sat down
and refused to budge. Three dogs
sniffed rather longer than was polite.
One goat jollied a lamb with his horn,
and one very small hamster left an
even smaller wet spot on the rug.

Emily saw it all because she leaned
over sideways and looked down the
aisle.

One by one the animals stood in front
of the pastor to be blessed. Last in
line was the difficult pig.

After he was blessed, he waddled
away looking pleased with himself.

When the service was over, everyone stood to leave. Emily stood, too, but instead of heading for the door, she tore down the aisle like a red dart. She didn't look back when her parents called. She headed straight for the altar, ducking purses and dodging elbows the whole way.

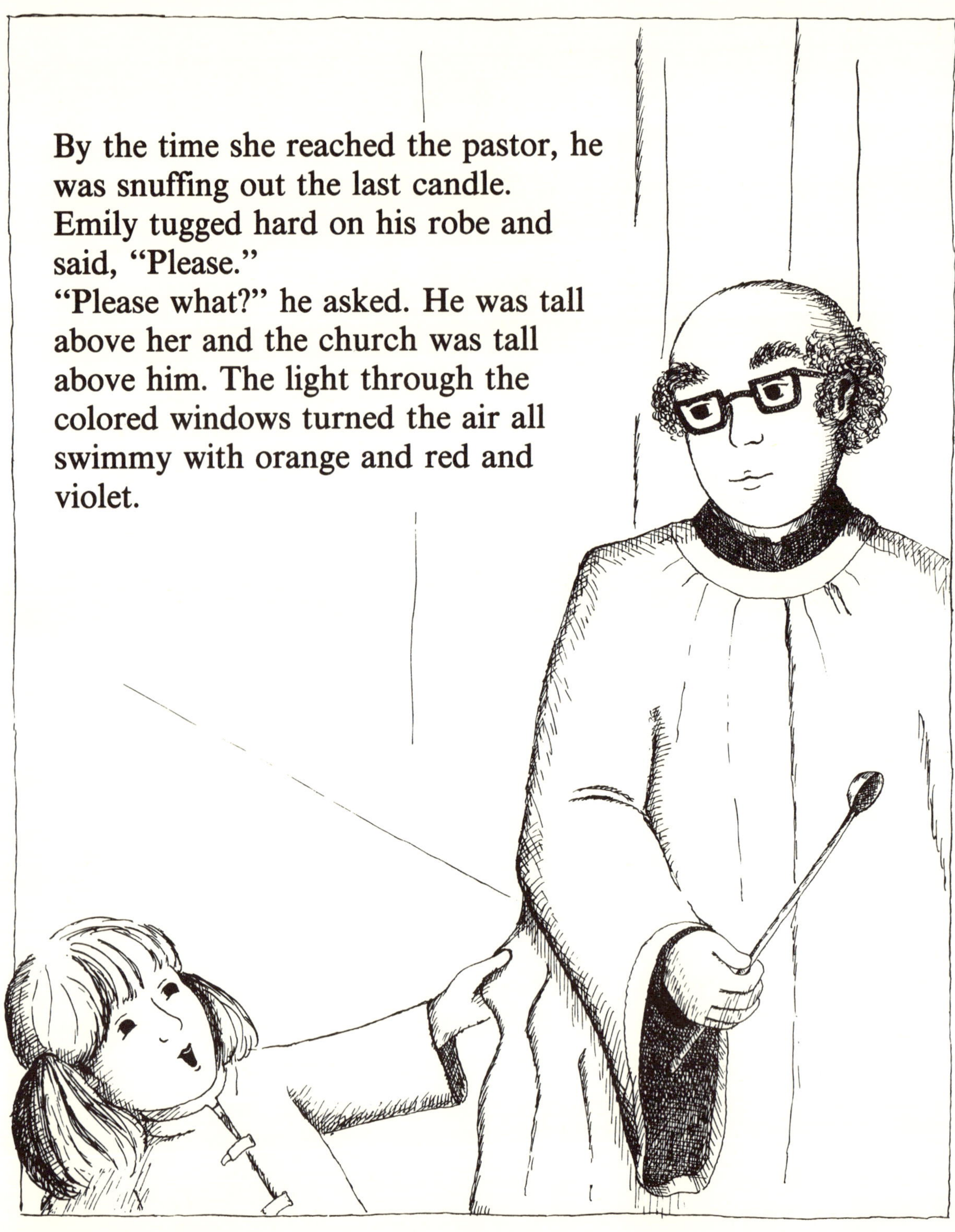

By the time she reached the pastor, he
was snuffing out the last candle.
Emily tugged hard on his robe and
said, "Please."
"Please what?" he asked. He was tall
above her and the church was tall
above him. The light through the
colored windows turned the air all
swimmy with orange and red and
violet.

"Please bless Tiger," Emily said.
"He's had a terrible quarrel." She
pulled Tiger's body from one pocket
of her raincoat and his right arm from
another.

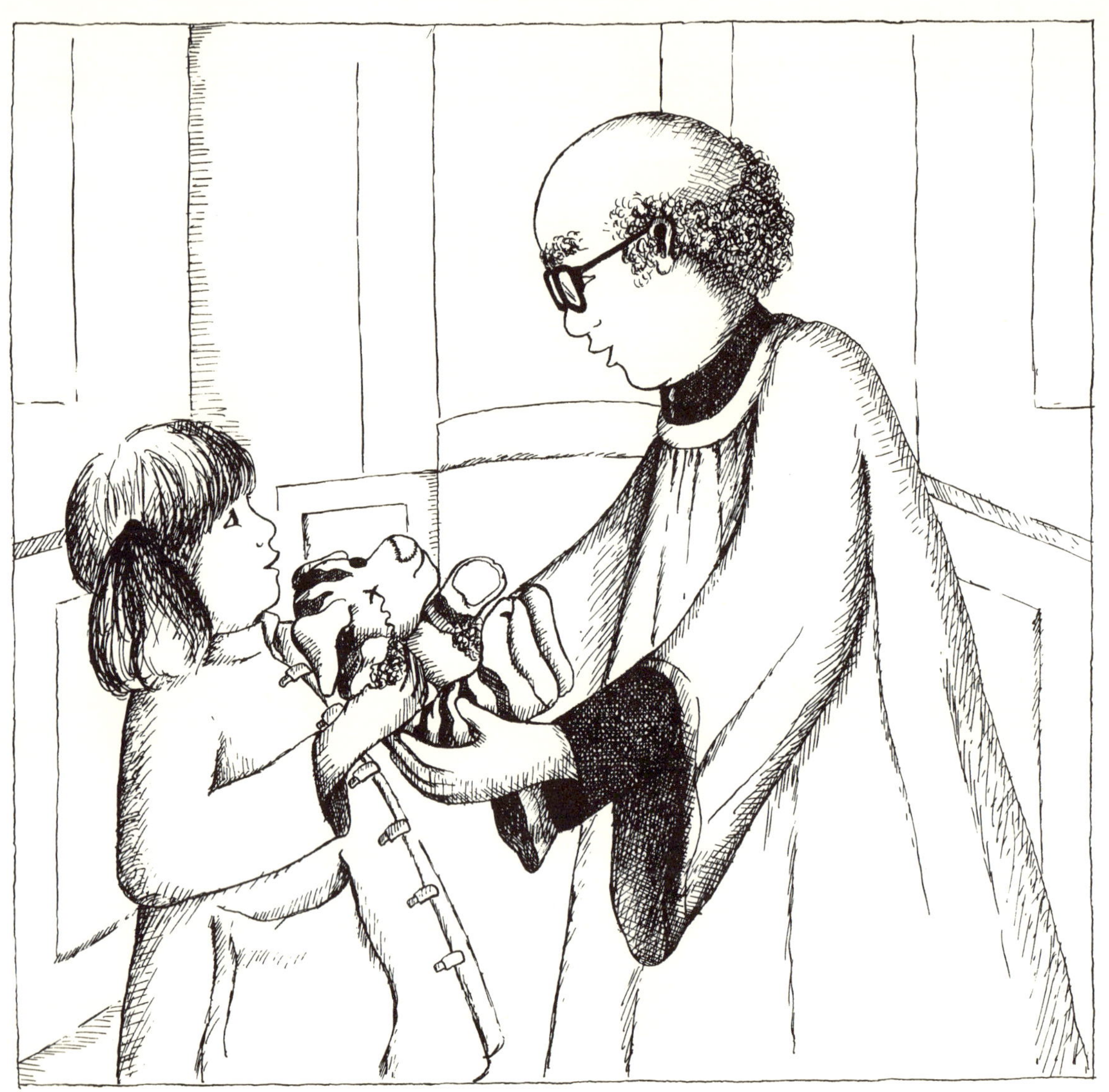

The pastor looked at lumpy Tiger and
said, "The Blessing is for real
animals."
"But Tiger is real," Emily said.
The man smiled and shook his head,
"No."

Emily rushed on, "Tiger shares my
pillow, he keeps my secrets, he says
his prayers and he really . . ."
"Wait," the man said, holding up the
candle snuffer. "How do you know he
says his prayers?"

"We say them together," Emily
explained. "And someday he wants to
be a policeman like my dad."
"I understand," the pastor said. He
laid down the snuffer and raised both
his hands over Tiger's head—and
Emily's—and said some soft words.
"Thank you," Emily said. "Thank
you for helping Tiger."

Her family was waiting at the back of
the church. They were quiet on the
way home.

But when they reached their house, her brother said, "Would old raggedy Tiger like Roscoe's ribbon?"
"Yes," said Emily.

"Do you think he could use two of my policeman buttons for eyes?" her father asked.
"Yes," said Emily.

"Shall I sew him now or after lunch?" her mother asked.
"Now," said Emily. "It's hard to eat lunch when you've got the lumps and your insides show."

Tiger never was cured of the lumps,
but he looked perfectly fine all the
same.

And he never camped out alone under
the lilac bush again. Emily saw to
that.